THE BREATHING BOOK

CHRISTOPHER WILLARD * OLIVIA WEISSER
* Art by ALISON OLIVER

sounds true
BOULDER, COLORADO

Welcome to *The Breathing Book*!

When you learn to understand and use your breath, it can do amazing things! It can reset your body when it feels stressed or out of control. It can help you focus your thoughts. It can help you relax.

Your breath is always with you. Take a moment and see how your breath feels right now.

This book will help you get to know your breath better and learn how to use it to feel happier and healthier.

Start by sitting comfortably.
Hold the book gently in your lap.

How does it feel?
Warm or cold?
Smooth or rough?
Light or heavy?

Run your fingers over the cover. Feel the edges
and corners of your book. Listen to the sounds
as you carefully turn the pages.

Look, a square!

You can begin to practice breathing with this.

Trace your finger along one side of the square while you breathe in, counting in your head *one, two, three, four*. Then trace your finger along the next side while holding your breath and counting in your head *one, two, three, four*. Now trace your finger along the next side while breathing out for four counts. Then trace the last side while holding your breath for four counts.

How do you feel after tracing the square?
How about after tracing the square four times?

These squiggly lines are breathing waves.
Trace these lines with your finger. Breathe in as
you go up, and breathe out as you go down.

How does your breath feel as you trace the
different lines?

How does your body feel?

Great, now turn the page.

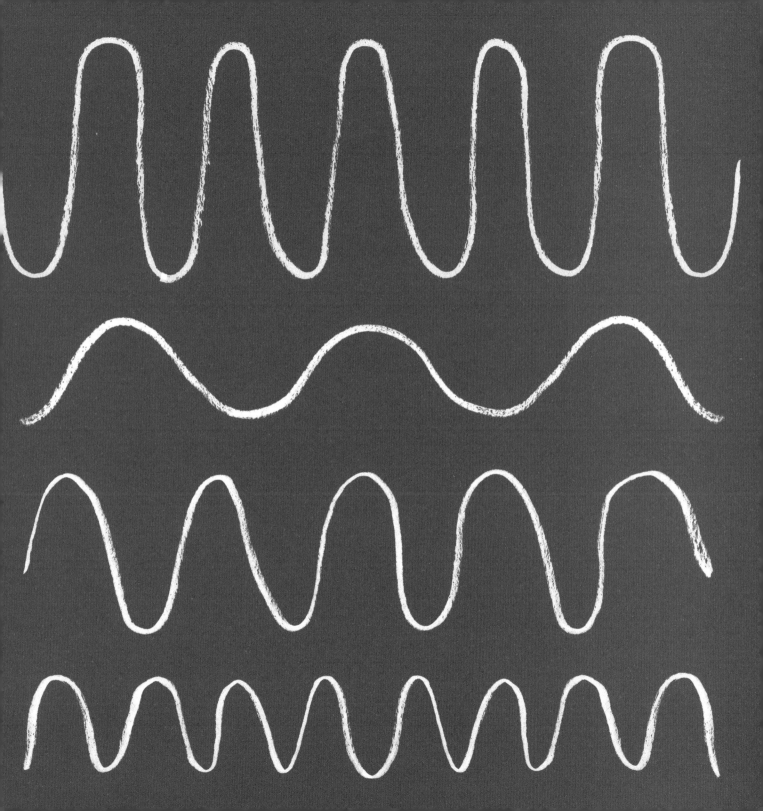

Okay, now lie down on your back and rest
the book on your belly. Are you comfortable?

Take three deep and slow breaths, keeping the
book balanced. Feel the book go up and down
on your belly as you breathe in and breathe out.

Great job!

Now we are going to get a page of the book
to stand up straight. Take a page between your
finger and thumb and hold it so it's standing up
straight, with the other pages lying flat on each
side. Now let go and gently blow on the page
to keep it from falling down.

Slow and steady! Don't let it fall over until the end
of your breath. You can keep practicing this as
long as you want.

You've turned the page again. How many page turns has that been? Can you remember?

Go back and turn the page again, this time really listening to the sound of the page turning. Where is the sound coming from?

Go back and take ten whole seconds to turn this page, trying to make no sound at all as you turn it.

Can you hear your breath?

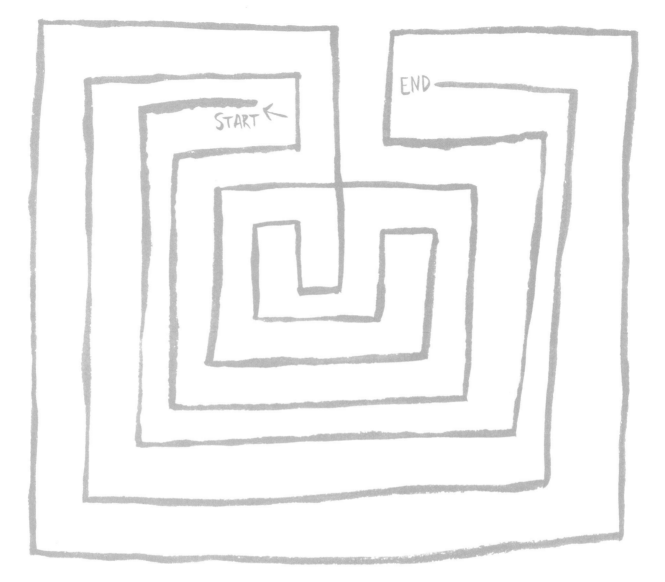

START

END

Trace one labyrinth all the way from the beginning
to the end with one finger. Breathe in while you do.
Then trace it from the end back to the beginning.
Breathe out while you do.

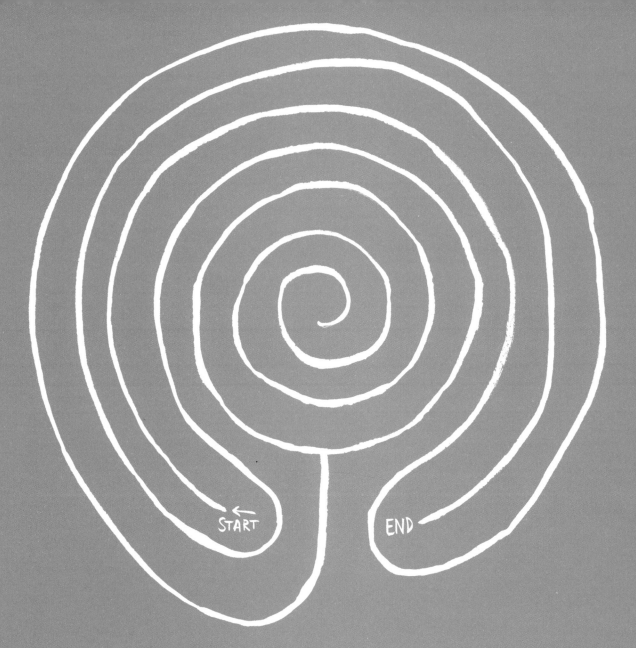

START

END

Now try tracing this labyrinth using a finger on your other hand. Can you do it silently? Can you do it while holding your breath? Can you trace both labyrinths at the same time, using both hands?

See this picture frame? Imagine putting a worry inside the frame. Now hold it up close to your face. It's hard to see much else, isn't it?

Now breathe out, pushing the frame away. Can you see more around it now?

Breathe out again and push it farther still, holding the book at arm's length. Notice the rest of the room around the book. Does your worry seem smaller now?

Even if you have a big worry, you can always draw a frame, put your worry in it, and then put it away somewhere.

Okay, now turn to the person reading this book with you. If you are reading it by yourself, imagine reading it with a friend.

Can you see or hear them breathing?

Try to match your breath with theirs so you are breathing in and out together.

Now balance the book flat on the palm of your hand. Pay attention. Is it easier when you breathe in or when you breathe out? Try to keep the book as still as you can while you focus on your breathing. For an added challenge, try balancing the book on the tips of your fingers.

Can you balance the book on your head?

Place your left hand flat on top of the outline. With your right pointer finger, trace around your left hand.

Breathe in as you trace your finger up, and out as you trace your finger down, until you've traced your whole hand. Now try the same thing switching hands.

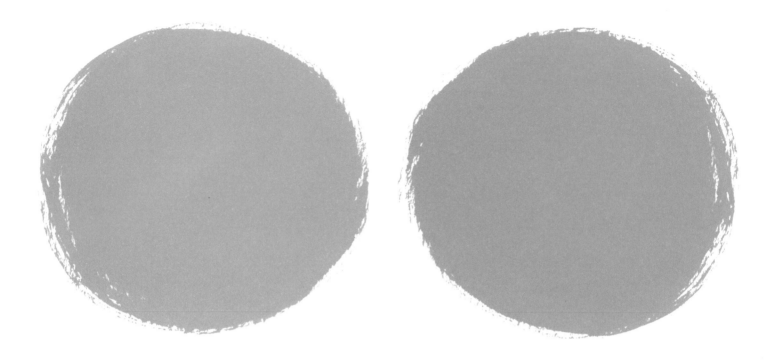

For the next few moments, let's just focus on your breathing.

Feel your breath going all the way in and all the way out.

Every time you notice yourself thinking about something besides your breathing, press one of the dots.

After you press the last dot, turn the page.

Now we will tie your breath to wishes.
These are kind wishes, okay?

Breathe in as you think of someone you
want to send a wish to.

Think of a wish.

Breathe out as you send them the wish.

Make a kind wish
for yourself.

Make a kind wish
for a friend.

Now make a wish
for the whole world.

Make a kind wish
for someone who
takes care of you.

This time make
a kind wish for
your community.

Take a deep breath in and let it all the way back out as you slowly close the book, finishing the breath when it's closed.

How does your breath feel now?
How do you feel?

Remember, you can use your breath to feel peaceful, focused, and happy!

To Mae and Leo
—CW and OW

To Hope
—AO

Sounds True
Boulder, CO 80306

Published 2020

Book design by Ranée Kahler
Cover design by Rachael Murray
Cover illustration by Alison Oliver

Printed in South Korea

Library of Congress Cataloging-in-Publication Data

Names: Willard, Christopher (Psychologist), author.
Title: The breathing book / by Christopher Willard and Olivia Weisser.
Description: Boulder, CO : Sounds True, Inc., 2020. | Audience: Ages 4-8 |

Identifiers: LCCN 2019028337 (print) | LCCN 2019028338 (ebook) |
   ISBN 9781683643067 (hardback) | ISBN 9781683643074 (ebook)
Subjects: LCSH: Breathing exercises--Juvenile literature. |
   Respiration--Juvenile literature.
Classification: LCC RA782 .W53 2020 (print) | LCC RA782 (ebook) |
   DDC 613/.192--dc23
LC record available at https://lccn.loc.gov/2019028337
LC ebook record available at https://lccn.loc.gov/2019028338

10 9 8 7 6 5 4 3 2 1